Tallulah's Ice Skates

by MARILYN SINGER

Illustrations by
ALEXANDRA BOIGER

CLARION BOOKS

Houghton Mifflin Harcourt | Boston | New York

Thanks to Cara Gargano and Paige Ketsoglou for their expert ballet and ice skating advice; to Steve Aronson for listening; to Alexandra Boiger for her great illustrations; and to my wonderful editor Jennifer Greene and everyone at Clarion/HMH.

Clarion Books
3 Park Avenue
New York, New York 10016

Clarion Books is an imprint of Houghton Mifflin Harcourt Publishing Company.

hmhco.com

The illustrations in this book were executed in watercolor and watercolor mixed with gouache and egg yolk, on Fabriano watercolor paper.
The text was set in Pastonchi MT Std.

Library of Congress Cataloging-in-Publication Data
Names: Singer, Marilyn, author.
Title: Tallulah's ice skates / by Marilyn Singer ; illustrated by Alexandra Boiger.
Description: Boston ; New York : Clarion Books, [2018] | Summary:
When Tallulah goes ice skating with her brother, Beckett, and best friend, Kacie, she learns that having fun can be more important than being the best.
Identifiers: LCCN 2018006983 | ISBN 9780544596924 (hardback)
Subjects: | CYAC: Ice skating—Fiction. | Play—Fiction. | Friendship—Fiction. |
BISAC: JUVENILE FICTION / Sports & Recreation / Ice Skating. |
JUVENILE FICTION / Humorous Stories. | JUVENILE FICTION /
Performing Arts / Dance. | JUVENILE FICTION / Social Issues /
Emotions & Feelings. | JUVENILE FICTION / Social Issues / Friendship.
| JUVENILE FICTION / Girls & Women.
Classification: LCC PZ7.S6172 Tad 2018 | DDC [E]—dc23
LC record available at https://lccn.loc.gov/2018006983

Manufactured in China
SCP 10 9 8 7 6 5 4 3 2 1
4500720310

To Jean Lerner and Liz Salen and their kids
—M.S.

To Lada, Lena, and Rose, with love
—A.B.

TALLULAH loved ballet class. But today she was glad when her lesson finished. Bluegill Pond was frozen over at last, and she and her friend Kacie were going skating!

Kacie was better at tap than Tallulah. But Tallulah was better at ballet. I'm sure we're both great at skating, Tallulah said to herself, smoothing down her red velvet skirt. After all, skating's a lot like dancing.

Her skirt wasn't quite as special as her tutu, but it would twirl beautifully when she did her perfect spin—which she planned to do that very day. If we practice enough, we might even get to be in an ice show.

"Are you ready already?" asked her brother, Beckett.

"Yes!" Tallulah said.

"Let's go!"

It was a good thing that the pond was big. There were a lot of skaters trying out all kinds of moves. The crows perched nearby on the bare maple tree limbs scolded them. Beckett scolded them back.

Tallulah rolled her eyes.

"There's Kacie and her mom!" said Tallulah.

"Have fun," said Tallulah's mom. "But don't try
any fancy stuff. I'll be sitting on this bench drinking
hot cocoa. That's *my* favorite winter sport."

Tallulah skated over to her friend. "Now presenting
the Super Skaters!" she announced. "Watch them spiral!
Watch them spin!"

"Watch them bunny hop!" Kacie exclaimed,
grabbing Tallulah's hand.

Tallulah and Kacie bunny hopped away. Beckett
skated next to them, swinging his arms too wide
and yelling, "Whee!" as loudly as he could.

Bunny hopping was fun for a while, but soon Tallulah wanted to try some fancier moves. "Let's do lunges together," she said.

"Lunches?" Kacie looked confused.

"No, *lunges*. Like this." She bent her front leg and stretched her other leg behind her and glided forward.

Kacie tried—and had to put her hands down on the ice.

"Do it again. Go a little faster and don't look down!" Tallulah said.

Once more, Kacie had to stop herself from falling. "Let's go back to bunny hopping," she said.

"Bunny hopping is for beginners, not Super Skaters," Tallulah said.

"So what?" said Kacie. "It's fun!"

"I'll bunny hop with you, Kacie," Beckett said.

Tallulah sighed. "Go ahead." Then she added, "But I'm going to practice my spin," and she glided away to the other side of the pond.

First, she did some swizzles, pointing her feet in and out in a *V* shape.

Then she tried some turns. Her skirt *did* whirl beautifully, but it would whirl even *more* beautifully when she did her perfect spin.

She extended her left arm in front of her and pressed the tip of her skate into the ice. Now presenting that graceful Super Skater—the one, the only, Tallulah!

She took a deep breath and
started to twirl.

But instead of spinning gracefully, she wobbled.
A lot.

"You can't skate on your tiptoes," someone said.

Tallulah looked over her shoulder.

Gliding around her in circles on one leg with both arms
outstretched was a boy a few years older than she was.

"You have to put your whole foot down," he went on.
"This is ice skating, not ballet."

"How did you know I dance ballet?" Tallulah asked.

"All you ballet girls make the same mistakes.
Go ahead, try it again."

"Humph," said Tallulah.
Then she tried again—
and wobbled once more.

"You've got a lot of work to do if you want
to get good." He pulled one leg up high behind
his head and twirled quickly on one foot. Then
he skated away.

"Good? Skating's a lot like ballet, and in ballet,
I'm better than good, Skater Boy!" she hollered
after him. "I can even do a perfect *sauté arabesque*!
Watch this!"

Planting her left toe on the ice, she leaped
into the air, lifting her right leg behind her.
For a brief moment, it felt wonderful—
and Tallulah was sure it looked wonderful too.

But instead of coming back down on her toe,
she landed on her heel and fell with a thump
on her rear end.

For a long moment, she just sat there.
Caw caw went the crows. To Tallulah, it
sounded as if they were laughing at her.

Tallulah's mom jumped up from the bench and cried, "Tallulah, are you all right?" Kacie and Beckett skated over as fast as they could, but Kacie's mother was faster. She helped Tallulah get up. "Are you hurt?" she asked.

Tallulah stared down at her skates. "No," she said quietly. She was sure Skater Boy was watching. "No, I'm not hurt," she repeated more loudly. But she was glad when it was time to go home.

The next day, Tallulah did not want to go skating at all. But Beckett did, and so they went to the pond. Tallulah pulled on her skates slowly.

"Aren't you excited to skate today?" her mother asked.

"Not really," said Tallulah, and she sat down on the bench.

"Well, today, *I* am," said her mom, handing Tallulah her cup of cocoa.

Tallulah watched her skate off with Beckett, both of them giggling as her mother tried to stay upright. They were not Super Skaters, but they looked like they were having fun.

I'm not a Super Skater either, Tallulah thought sadly. She missed the swooshy sound her skates made and the way the cool air tingled on her face.

Then she saw Kacie. Kacie gave a little wave. Tallulah hesitated, then waved back.

Kacie skated over, but just as she reached Tallulah, Skater Boy appeared.

"Ballet Girl, what are you doing on the bench?" he asked in a friendly voice. "Don't you want to try your spin again?"

"My spin?" Tallulah was surprised. But she
was glad he didn't mention her jump.
    "You know, you're not so bad, and you
really will get better if you practice."

"We practice all the time," Kacie told him.
"Today, we're here to have fun." She held out
her hand and pulled Tallulah up.

And then Tallulah knew just what she wanted to do.
"Maybe I'll practice later," Tallulah said to the boy. "But right now,
my friend and I are going to bunny hop." She smiled at Kacie.

"And lunge," Kacie added, smiling back.

"And then LUNCH," they both said at the same time.

Then, linking arms, they bunny hopped away, yelling "Whee!" as loudly as they could.

Simple Spin